William D. Malton

The ABC of Skirmishing

AF141193

SALZWASSER
VERLAG

William D. Malton

The ABC of Skirmishing

Reprint of the original, first published in 1859.

1st Edition 2022 | ISBN: 978-3-37512-062-7

Verlag (Publisher): Salzwasser Verlag GmbH, Zeilweg 44, 60439 Frankfurt, Deutschland
Vertretungsberechtigt (Authorized to represent): E. Roepke, Zeilweg 44, 60439 Frankfurt, Deutschland
Druck (Print): Books on Demand GmbH, In de Tarpen 42, 22848 Norderstedt, Deutschland

THE

A B C

OF

SKIRMISHING:

BEING THE

LIGHT INFANTRY MOVEMENTS OF A COMPANY.

IN ACCORDANCE WITH

THE FIELD EXERCISE AND EVOLUTIONS OF INFANTRY. 1859.

BY

WILLIAM D. MALTON, M.A.,

LATE 2ND ROYAL MIDDLESEX RIFLES.

(Author of " Company and Battalion Drill Illustrated.")

LONDON:

PRINTED AND PUBLISHED BY

W. CLOWES AND SONS, 14, CHARING CROSS.

1859.

PREFACE.

———

This little work is published under the idea that a short Manual of reference on Elementary Light Drill may, at the present time, be found useful.

The language of the *Field Exercise*, than which nothing could be more clear or concise, has been closely adhered to throughout.

May 1859.

CONTENTS.

GENERAL PRINCIPLES

OF

SKIRMISHING.

SKIRMISHERS, SUPPORTS, AND RESERVES.

(1) *Skirmishers.*

THE movements of Skirmishers must depend, in a great measure, on the position and movements of the Enemy : they should always, however, protect and over-lap the flanks of the main body they are intended to cover.

Skirmishers (whether halted or in motion) when under fire, should take advantage of all cover: taking care, when advancing or retiring, not to get in front of each other, or to retain their places of cover so long as to interfere with their own or their comrades' fire.

All lines of Skirmishers move by their *centre:* except when inclining to a flank (p. 20), in which case they move by the flank to which they are inclining.

The distance between Skirmishers and Supports, on a plain, should be about 240 paces.

Whenever Skirmishers are directed to HALT (whether by word of command or by bugle sound), they will halt and *kneel,* facing to their proper front.

N.B.—Men in extended order will invariably face (or turn) to the *right-*about; whether advancing, retiring, firing, or not firing : when one man of a file has to pass the other, he will always pass him by the *proper* left.

Rules for Skirmishers firing.—The men of a file must always work together. Both men should never be unloaded at the same time: the loaded man is always nearest the Enemy. Men should always load, when practicable, under cover.

When Skirmishers (either halted or on the march,) are directed to CEASE FIRING, they will complete their loading; and the rear-rank men, if not already there, will resume their places in the proper rear of their respective front-rank men.

It should be recollected that CEASE FIRING *is the only sound that annuls the* FIRE.

(2) *Supports.*

The Supports should always be composed of numbers equal to the line of Skirmishers: thus, each Company that is extended should have a Company to support it; and in the case of a single Company detached to skirmish, one Subdivision should skirmish while the other remains formed in support.

It is the duty of the Supports to assist the Skirmishers (with whose movements their own will correspond) in every possible way; availing themselves, at the same time, of any cover that may present itself.

Supports take ground to a flank by Sections: if moving diagonally to the front or rear, they move in echellon of Sections. (*Field Ex.*, p. 71.)

Each Support should be in rear of the centre of its own Skirmishers.

The distance between Supports and Reserves, on a plain, should be about 360 paces.

Both Skirmishers and Supports move with *trailed* Arms: except when moving into close column of Sections (p. 28), or when marching in File; on which occasions they will necessarily *shoulder*.

(3) *Reserves.*

The Reserve is the point on which both Supports and Skirmishers may rally : and should be, at least, one-third of the whole body. It will be placed as nearly as possible in rear of the centre of the formation, in order to send relief to the Supports and Skirmishers, as occasion may require.

In the presence of Cavalry, the Reserve should be kept in column ; but under the fire of Artillery should be *deployed* into line. (*Field Ex.*, p. 163.)

Reserves take ground to a flank by fours : if moving obliquely to front or rear, they move by the diagonal march [RIGHT (or LEFT) HALF TURN].

The Reserve will be about 600 paces from the main body.

Light Infantry movements will usually be performed in Quick time : but extensions (or closings) *on the march*, the formation of Company- or Rallying-Squares, and changes of front from the halt, will be in Double time. [In Quick time, 108 30-inch steps (= 90 yards) : in Double time, 150 36-inch steps (= 150 yards) : are taken in a minute.]

OFFICERS.

1. When a Company is *extended,* the Captain will be in rear of the centre : the Lieutenant, in rear of the right : the Ensign, in rear of the left.

[The Lieutenant of a *flank* Company will always be in rear of its outer flank, whether that flank is the right or left : the Ensign, in rear of the inner flank.]

2. When a Company (whether advancing or retiring) is in *support,* the Captain is always in its *proper* front ; leading the

Company when it advances, following it when it retires. The Lieutenant and Ensign will be in the proper rear.

The Officer commanding a Support should—with due regard to the assistance he should afford the Skirmishers—take advantage of all inequalities of ground to get his men under cover; making them lie down if necessary. The best positions to select are those which will protect the men if attacked by Cavalry, without preventing the Skirmishers forming on them.

3. The Officers of a *Reserve* will always be placed as in column, *right* in front: *i.e.*, the Captains on the left of the front rank, the Lieutenants one pace in rear of the 2d file from the right, the Ensigns one pace in rear of the centre, of their respective Companies.

The Officer commanding the Reserve, without forgetting to avail himself of cover when practicable, should chiefly direct his attention to the selection of positions favourable to the relief and assistance of the Skirmishers and Supports: with due regard to the protection of the main body.

BUGLE SOUNDS.

One G denotes the right
Two G's denote the centre ⎬ of the line.
Three G's ,, the left

The G (or G's) preceding any sound denote the part of the line to which the sound applies.

E.g. Two G's sounded before the EXTEND signify to extend from the centre: one G followed by the CLOSE will signify to close to the right; three G's followed by the WHEEL, to wheel to the left.

N.B. The HALT annuls all previous sounds except the FIRE. When the FIRE is combined with any other call, it should always be the last of the two.

Bugle sounds do not apply to bodies of troops in reserve.

When moving by sound of bugle, men will wait till the bugle has ceased before they move.

[The numbers affixed to the Sounds in this book correspond with those in the *Field Exercise*, pp. 210–212.]

*** The directions given for *shouldering* Arms, and fixing *swords*, apply to the short Rifle.

LIGHT INFANTRY MOVEMENTS OF A COMPANY.

The Company will fall in in two ranks (each rank sized from flanks to centre) at *close* order *, with ordered Arms; the files lightly touching : and, having been numbered from right to left, will be told off into 2 Subdivisions and 4 Sections.

The left file of the right Subdivision will always be considered the centre of the Company. (*Field Ex.*, p. 49.)

SEC. I.—EXTENDING.

[The numbers of paces that the files are to extend from each other may be specified in the *caution* by the Commander, thus : —THREE PACES, FROM THE RIGHT—EXTEND. When no number of paces is specified, 6 paces will be the distance between files. The rear-rank man of each file is responsible for distance : the front-rank man for direction.]

N.B. In extending from the Halt, each (except the named) file will face to the right or left as the case may be, and move off in Quick time : in extending on the March, it will make only a *half* turn, and will move off in Double time.

(1) *Extending from the Halt.*

FROM THE RIGHT (LEFT, CENTRE, or No.—FILE): EXTEND.

[CALL 1.]

On the word (or *Sound*) EXTEND—

The *Officers* fall to the rear. (See p. 9.)

The file on the named flank (or the centre- or named file) kneels down : the remainder shoulder Arms, face outwards, and extend in Quick time.

---

* *i.e.* with the rear rank distant one pace from the front rank, measuring from heel to heel.

The front-rank men move direct to the flank to which they have faced, covering correctly on the march. The rear-rank men will cast their eyes over the inward shoulder; and each, as he gains the proper distance, will tap his front-rank man on the shoulder as a signal, and both men will halt, front, and kneel.

[Men must be taught to extend from any file of a close column of Sections (*see* p. 28), without previously re-forming Company: the named file will kneel, and the remainder (having faced outwards) will extend as above.]

(2) *Extending on the March.*

On the word (or *Sound*) EXTEND—

The file from which the extension is to be made continues to move straight forward in Quick time.

The remainder will make a *half* turn outwards, and move off in Double time: each file turning to its front and resuming the Quick time, when it has gained the required distance; the rear-rank men covering their front-rank men; and the whole keeping in line with the directing (centre) file.

N.B.—If the Company is ordered to HALT before all the files are extended, the remainder will make another *half* turn outwards (which will bring them into file), break into Quick time, shoulder Arms, and complete their extension as from the Halt.

Men in extended order may be directed to increase the distance between their files any given number of paces; from either flank, the centre, or any named file.

If the extension is ordered by bugle sound, or if no number of paces is specified in the word of command, the Skirmishers will open out *one half* more than their original extension ; *e.g.*, if they are at 6 paces distance, they will open to 9 paces.

N.B.—Officers in command of Skirmishers should be able to judge the number of paces it is necessary to extend, in order to cover the front of a *Line*. When the extent of the front is known, one pace should be allowed for each file of the Line : thus—To cover the front, and over-lap the flanks of, 360 files (each file having a front of 21 inches), a Company of Skirmishers consisting of 40 files should, in extending, divide 360 paces : *i.e.*, the files should extend 9 paces from each other.

See *Field Exercise*, pp. 213-215.

Sec. II.—CLOSING.

(1) *Closing at the Halt.*

ON THE RIGHT (LEFT, CENTRE, or No.— FILE): CLOSE.

[CALL II.]

On the word (or *Sound*) CLOSE—

The file on the named flank (or the centre- or named file) will rise, order Arms, and stand at ease.

The remainder will rise, face towards the file on which the closing is to be made, and close in Quick time; each file in succession halting, fronting, ordering Arms, and standing at ease, as it gets to its place.

The *Officers* will remain in rear, unless directed to take post as in Company.

[The file on which the Skirmishers close may be faced in any direction: the remainder forming upon it accordingly.]

(2) *Closing on the March.*

On the word (or *Sound*) CLOSE—

The file on which the closing is to be made will move steadily on in Quick time: the remainder making a *half* turn towards it; closing in Double time; and turning to the front and resuming the Quick time, as they get to their places.

N.B.—If the Company is ordered to HALT before all the files are closed, the remainder will make a second *half* turn inwards (which will bring them into file), break into Quick time, and complete the closing as from the Halt.

See *Field Exercise,* p. 215.

Sec. III.—FIRING IN SKIRMISHING ORDER, AT THE HALT.

COMMENCE FIRING.

[CALL V.]

On the word (or *Sound*) COMMENCE FIRING—

The front-rank men will make ready, fire, and re-load: the rear-rank men, when their respective front-rank men are in the act of capping, will make ready, fire, and re-load.

———

A line of Skirmishers may be ordered to *lie down*, or single soldiers may lie down for the sake of cover: when firing in this position, both elbows must rest on the ground to support the body and rifle. The men will load on their knees: except in very exposed situations, when they may roll over on their backs, placing the butt of the rifle between the legs, lock upwards, and muzzle slightly elevated.

[Riflemen may, in favourable situations, fire while on their backs: the feet being crossed, and the right foot passed through the sling of the rifle to support it.]

When a line of Skirmishers halted is ordered to *advance* or *retire* firing, the front-rank men will first fire: the whole will then rise, and proceed as explained in the two following Sections.

See *Field Exercise*, p. 220.

Sec. IV.—ADVANCING IN SKIRMISHING ORDER, AND FIRING.

COMPANY: ADVANCE.

[CALL III.]

On the word (or *Sound*) ADVANCE—

The men will rise, and step off in Quick time.

On the word (or *Sound*) COMMENCE FIRING—

The whole of the Skirmishers will make a momentary halt; the front-rank man of each file will then fire (kneeling, if he prefers it), and take a side pace to his left. The rear-rank man will then pass on, the front-rank man following close in rear of him, loading on the march. When in the act of capping, the front-rank man will give the word "Ready" in an under tone of voice; on which the proper rear-rank man will fire. Both men will then proceed, alternately, as above described.

The loaded man in front is responsible for distance and dressing.

[When men find difficulty in loading on the march, they may *halt* and load, and then double up to their file leaders.]

The men must take advantage of any cover that may offer, running from one place to another as soon as they are loaded. When any considerable place of cover presents itself, several files may run up to it, fire and load, and then regain their distances and places in the general line of Skirmishers.

¶ *Passing obstacles in Skirmishing order.*

When an obstacle (such as a pond or marsh) presents itself in front of a line of Skirmishers, the files opposite to it will open out gradually as they approach, and will pass on either side of it; closing upon the remaining files, which will continue moving straight to their front. Having passed the obstacle, the files that have been impeded by it will again extend, and fill up the interval in the line.

A Company advancing, or retiring, in skirmishing order should also be practised in closing on *the centre files of Subdivisions or Sections;* those files continuing to march straight to their front: after which, the Company will be again extended from the same files, when the distances between the files ought to be found correct.

See *Field Exercise,* pp. 217, 220.

Sec. V.—RETIRING IN SKIRMISHING ORDER, AND FIRING.

COMPANY: RETIRE. — [CALL VIII.]

On the word (or *Sound*) RETIRE—

The men will rise, face to the right-about, and step off (in Quick time) rear rank in front.

On the word (or *Sound*) COMMENCE FIRING—

Both ranks will halt and front. The front-rank man of each file will then fire, face to the right about, and retire in Quick time; passing by the *left* of his rear-rank man, and loading as he retires. The rear-rank man of each file will follow close in rear of his front-rank man. As soon as the front-rank man's loading is completed, both men will halt and front: and the rear-rank man will give his fire, and proceed as above described.

The men who are retiring and re-loading are responsible for distance and dressing.

[On rough ground, files will run back from one place of cover to another, selecting new cover before leaving the last: one man of each file should fire previous to moving, and re-load when again under cover.]

See *Field Exercise*, pp. 217, 221.

Sec. VI.—INCLINING TO A FLANK, AND FIRING.

TO THE RIGHT (or LEFT): INCLINE.

[CALL IX: preceded by one G. or three G's.]

On the word (or *Sound*) INCLINE—

The Skirmishers will make a *half* turn to the ordered flank, and will move in a diagonal direction, till they are ordered to resume their original direction to the front [or rear] by the word (*or* Sound) ADVANCE [*or* RETIRE].

The leading file is the directing file.

If the Skirmishers have made a half turn, and are again ordered to incline in the same direction; or if the bugle sounds the INCLINE a second time; they will make a second half turn (thus completing the *turn*), and will take ground to the flank in file.

On the word (or *Sound*) COMMENCE FIRING—

The front-rank men will halt, take steady aim, and fire: the rear-rank men moving on. Having fired, the front-rank men will double up to the proper rear of their respective rear-rank men, and will then load on the march [or, they may load at the halt, and *then* double up].

The rear-rank men, when the front-rank men's loading is completed, will proceed in like manner.

The loaded men are responsible for distance and dressing.

The ADVANCE, or the RETIRE, sounded when men are inclining to a flank, will indicate, that the original direction is to be resumed.

If the HALT sounds, the men halt, *front*, and *kneel*.

See *Field Exercise*, pp. 218, 222.

Sec. VII.—SKIRMISHERS CHANGING FRONT, OR DIRECTION, FROM THE HALT.

[A line of Skirmishers may change front on any two named files placed as a base for the rest to form upon. The change of front may be made at any angle; but it is not likely to be required to a greater extent than $\frac{1}{16}$ or (at most) $\frac{1}{8}$ of a circle.]

(1) *From the Halt.*

CHANGE FRONT TO THE RIGHT (or LEFT) ON THE TWO CENTRE [or ON No. — AND No. —] FILES.

DOUBLE MARCH.

On the Caution —

The two named files will rise, and the Captain will dress them in the required direction: the files, when placed, will again kneel.

On the word MARCH—

The whole will rise.

(*a*) If all the files are to be thrown *forward* on a flank, they will make a half turn inwards, and move across (by the shortest way) to their places in the new line; dressing on the two base files, and then kneeling.

(*b*) If all the files are to be thrown *back* on either flank, they will make a three-quarters face in the direction of the base files: they will then move across, and (in succession) halt, front, and kneel, as they get to their places in the new line.

If the change of front is on two central files, part of the Company will be thrown forward, as in (*a*): the remainder will be thrown back, as in (*b*).

[Recruits should first be taught this movement in *Quick* time, and by separate words of command: thus, after placing the base files, the Instructor will give RISE. LEFT SUBDIVISION, RIGHT HALF FACE: RIGHT SUBDIVISION, LEFT ABOUT THREE-QUARTERS FACE. THE WHOLE: Q. MARCH.]

(2) *On the March.*

[A line of Skirmishers on the march may change their direction gradually, on the same principle as a Company wheeling on a moveable pivot.—*Field Ex.*, p. 30.]

SKIRMISHERS: RIGHT (*or* LEFT) WHEEL.

[CALL X: *preceded by one G, or three G's*].

FORWARD.

On the word (or *Sound*) WHEEL—

The pivot file will halt: and the remainder will circle round it; the front-rank men looking outwards for the dressing, and the rear-rank men keeping the distances from the pivot flank.

On the word FORWARD: the whole line will advance by the centre.

N.B.—When Skirmishers wheel while *retiring*, the proper rear-rank men are responsible for dressing, proper front-rank men for distance.

See *Field Exercise*, p. 218.

Sec. VIII.—RELIEVING SKIRMISHERS.

[Both this and the following Movement are given in the *Field Exercise*, under the head of MOVEMENTS OF THE BATTALION; but may be practised by a Company, one Subdivision skirmishing, the other acting as a Support.]

(1) *Relieving halted Skirmishers.*

RELIEVE SKIRMISHERS. The Support will extend in rear, and then run up to the line of Skirmishers.

The old Skirmishers, on being relieved, will run straight to their rear; close on the left file of the 1st or the right of the 4th Section, according as they belong to the right or left Subdivision; and become the Support.

(2) *Relieving Skirmishers that are advancing.*

The Support will extend on the march, and the men will then double up to the old Skirmishers, changing into Quick time as they pass through them.

The old Skirmishers will lie down till the new are sufficiently advanced to protect them from immediate fire: they will then rise, close as in (1), and form the Support.

(3) *Relieving Skirmishers that are retiring.*

The Support will halt, front, and extend at a considerable distance in rear; each man, if possible, getting under cover.

When the old Skirmishers arrive within 20 or 30 paces of the new, they will run through them to the rear, till out of immediate fire; they will then close, and form the Support as already explained.

¶ *Reinforcing Skirmishers.*

The Support (or part of it) will be thrown forward as in Relieving Skirmishers; but on joining the line of Skirmishers will remain, and skirmish, in it; the distances being divided. [When any portion of a line of Skirmishers is called in, they will retire in the same manner as relieved Skirmishers; the remaining Skirmishers dividing the space left by those who have retired.]

N.B.—The Commander of the Support, when he brings it up to the Skirmishers, must call out that he is come to *relieve* or *reinforce* them, as the case may be, that the Commander of the latter may know how to act.

See *Field Exercise,* pp. 230-232.

Sec. IX.—CLOSING ON THE SUPPORT.

(1) *The Close.*

CLOSE ON SUPPORT.

[CALL II.]

The Skirmishers rise, face to the right about, and retire; the inner files of Sections moving at Quick time, and so as to clear the flanks of the Support, the remainder closing on those files as they retire.

When at Section distance in rear of the Support, the Sections will turn inwards, shouldering Arms as they turn. As the Sections meet (in rear of the Support), they will halt and front, order Arms, and stand at ease, without any word of command.

(2) *The Close and Alarm.*

CLOSE. LOOK OUT FOR CAVALRY.

[CALL II: *followed by* CALL XI.]

The Support will advance, forming Sections on the march (*Field Ex.*, p. 80): and the Skirmishers will move to the rear at the double; closing on the inward files of Sections as in (1), except that the centre files will incline outwards as they commence retiring, in order to clear the front of the Support.

As the Skirmishers approach the Support, the latter will halt, its rear Section closing on its leading Section, and both Sections fixing swords as they come to the halt.

The Skirmishers then turn inwards, so as to form close column of Sections with the Support (*see* p. 29), fixing swords as they halt and front.

The two Subdivisions will then be ordered to prepare for Cavalry (*see* p. 29).

When the EXTEND sounds, the old Support will advance and extend from the centre, thus becoming the new Skirmishers; the old Skirmishers will form Sub-division in support. Or, the old Support may extend *from the halt* on its own ground; the old Skirmishers re-forming Subdivision, and retiring to their proper distance as the Support.

See *Field Exercise,* p. 234.

Sec. X.—SQUARES.

(A) Company Squares.

From close order.

[In forming from *close* order (*i.e.* when not extended), the men will move into column with shouldered Arms: the Section of formation (No. 2) fixing swords at the word MARCH; the remainder, as they halt and front in column.]

(From Close order)
FORM CLOSE
COLUMN OF
SECTIONS.

Q. MARCH.

(1) *On the word* SECTIONS—

The 1st Section faces to the left, and disengages to the front (by the leading file closing 2 paces outwards): the 3rd and 4th Sections face to the right, and disengage (in like manner) to the rear.

The 2d Section stands fast.

(2) *On the word* MARCH—

Close column is formed on the 2d Section: the men halting and fronting, as they arrive in column, without word of command. The distance between the Sections will be one pace.

The *Captain* places himself on the left of the front rank of the leading Section: the *Lieutenant* and *Ensign* will be on the right flanks of the 3rd and 4th Sections respectively.

[The men should count the steps they have to take in getting into column: so that, in re-forming Company, the men of the 1st Section may turn to the rear; those of the 3rd and 4th Sections, to the front; together.]

From extended order.

The men order Arms and fix swords, independently, as they halt and front in their places.

[A Company must be practised in closing from extended order into close column of Sections, *on any named file*: when no file is named, the men will close on the left file of the 2nd Section. If much pressed by Cavalry, the first Section formed may commence firing; and the remainder may form in rear of it, the Sections passing each other left arm to left arm.]

If the INCLINE sounds while the men are in Square, they will shoulder their Arms; and face into, and move off in, the ordered direction.

Resisting Cavalry.

PREPARE FOR CAVALRY. — READY.

On the word CAVALRY—

The Officers and N. C. Officers move into the centre of the column: the men will then face outwards, so as to show a front of equal strength in every direction.

On the word READY—

If the Square is two or three-deep, the front rank only, will kneel: if four-deep, the 2 front ranks will kneel. The remainder come to the ' Ready.'

For firing words, *see* page 31.

Re-forming Company.

RE-FORM COLUMN. — RE-FORM COMPANY. — Q. MARCH.

On the word COLUMN—

The men will face to their proper front in column, and will touch into the pivot flanks. The Officers place themselves on the flanks of Sections.

On the word COMPANY—

Nos. 1, 3, and 4 Sections face outwards, and

On the word MARCH—

Move out: the 1st Section, when clear, turning to
the rear, the 3rd and 4th Sections (in succession) to
the front. Each of the three Sections will form up in
line with the 2nd Section without word of command:
the Officers taking post as with a Support.

(B) THE RALLYING SQUARE.

[This Square is for men of different Companies mixed together
in extended order, or for detached Skirmishers overtaken by
Cavalry.]

At the word SQUARE—

FORM RALLY-
ING SQUARE.

[CALL XI:
followed by
CALL XVI.]

The men will double up to the *nearest* Officer* standing as a rallying point: fixing swords, and ordering
Arms, as they reach him. The 2 first men who come
up to the Officer form on his right and left, facing outwards: the 3 next in front: the 3 next in rear, facing
to the rear.

The next 4 men place themselves one at each angle
of the Square thus formed: and others, as they come up,
complete the face between those angles.

After each completion of the faces of the Square, the
4 next men place themselves one at each angle: others
completing the faces as before.

[For PREPARE FOR CAVALRY, *see* next Section.]

See *Field Exercise*, pp. 84-87.

---

* Officers giving points for Skirmishers to form on, should
place themselves in Echellon with each other, so as not to mask
the fire of any face.

Sec. XI.—A SQUARE RECEIVING CAVALRY.

Prepare for Cavalry	2nd and 4th ranks take a pace of 9 inches to the front.
Ready	The 2 front ranks [or, in 2 deep Squares, the front rank only] will sink on the right knee, and place the butts of the rifles against the inside of that knee — locks uppermost, and muzzles slanted upwards.
Commence firing from the — of Faces	Standing rank(s) commence File firing thus :—The files fire in succession (front and rear-rank men alternately) from the named flank, for the 1st round : each file then loads and fires independently.
Cease firing . . .	Each file completes its loading and shoulders: those that are at the ' Ready ' first half-cocking their rifles.

Kneeling rank(s) :
fire a Volley

At — yards : Ready { Kneeling rank(s) will come to the capping position, adjust the sights, and full cock.

Present . . . . { After firing, the rifles are again brought down to receive Cavalry.

Load . . . . { The kneeling rank(s) will spring to Attention at the half face : come to the 'Prepare to load' position, and go on with the loading in Quick time.

THE END.

I. EXTEND.

II. CLOSE.

III. ADVANCE.

IV. HALT.

The *Halt* annuls all previous Sounds except the *Fire*.

V. COMMENCE FIRING.

VI. CEASE FIRING.

VII. RETIRE.

VIII ASSEMBLY.

This sound will be used to turn out troops in cases of alarm by day or night, *and for no other purpose.*

IX. Incline.

X. Wheel.

The calls IX and X must be preceded by the distinguishing G's.

XI. The Alarm, or Look out for Cavalry.

XII. The Officers' Call.

XIII. The Quick Time.

XIV. The Double Time.